The Railway Rabbits

Bracken Finds a Secret Tunnel

Orion
Children's Books

First published in Great Britain in 2011
by Orion Children's Books
a division of the Orion Publishing Group Ltd
Orion House
5 Upper St Martin's Lane
London WC2H 9EA
An Hachette UK Company

1 3 5 7 9 10 8 6 4 2

Text copyright © Georgie Adams 2011
Illustrations copyright © Anna Currey 2011

Printed in Great Britain by Clays Ltd, St. Ives plc.

ISBN 978 1 4440 0160 0

www.orionbooks.co.uk

The

Rabbits

Bracken Finds a Secret Tunnel

For my editor, Jenny Glencross,
with thanks for keeping the rabbits
hopping along!

G.A.

The Ripple River Valley

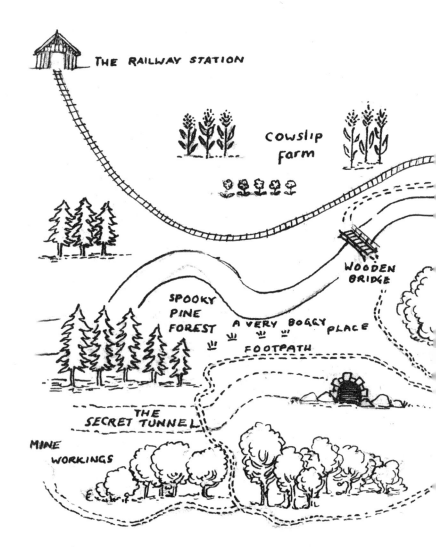

THE RAILWAY STATION

COWSLIP FARM

WOODEN BRIDGE

SPOOKY PINE FOREST

A VERY BOGGY PLACE

FOOTPATH

THE SECRET TUNNEL

MINE WORKINGS

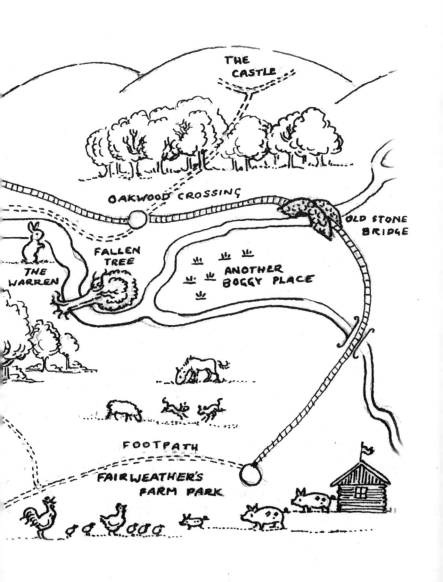

Lost in the Mist

1

Early one morning in autumn, a white mist hung over the River Ripple Valley where the Railway Rabbits lived. Bracken Longears was the first to hop out of the burrow and today he got quite a surprise. He couldn't see his paw in front of his nose.

"Slugs and snails!" cried Bracken. "What's happened? I can't see a thing.

Where are the trees? Where's the river?
Where has everything gone?"

Barley Longears, Bracken's parr,
hurried up-burrow to see what was
the matter.

"It's a weather thing," said Barley.
"It happens at this time of year. Don't
worry. The mist will soon clear."

Soon the rest of the Longears family
came hopping out of the burrow too.

First came Bramble, quickly followed
by Berry and Fern. Mellow, their marr,
was next to appear. Last came Wisher,
the smallest of the young rabbits. She
stretched and rubbed sleep from her eyes.

But when she opened them she couldn't see anyone, even though she could hear them talking.

"Where are you?" she said.

"Here!" said Berry.

"This way!" said Bramble.

"Over here!" said Fern.

"Right behind you!" said Bracken.

"Boo!"

"Bracken!" said Wisher, spinning round. "You made me jump!"

The others laughed. It was fun playing hide-and-seek in the mist, but Barley looked worried.

"You see how easily Bracken crept up on Wisher without being seen?" he said. "You must all be extra careful this morning. Your enemies could sneak up on you too."

"Ooo!" said Fern. "I hadn't thought of that."

Bramble looked puzzled.

"I know we should always be on the look-out for Burdock the buzzard or a fox, Parr," he said. "But we'll be all right today, won't we? If we can't see them, they can't see us!"

Barley scratched one ear, wondering what to say. Bramble was the biggest of his five young rabbits, and he was fearless. It sometimes led him into trouble.

"Our enemies may find it more difficult to hunt in the mist," said Barley. "But don't forget, Burdock can hear well, and a fox has a fine nose for smelling rabbits."

"Parr is right," said Mellow. "You must all look after each other. And don't go far. Remember, silly rabbits have careless habits!"

"I'll look after you, Wisher," said Bracken. "Come on. Let's find something to eat."

"I don't want to be on my own," said Fern.

"You can come with Berry and me," said Bramble.

"Only if you promise not to sneak up on me."

"We PROMISE!" they said.

For a while the five young rabbits stayed
together. But it wasn't long before the
two groups were separated in the mist.
Bracken and Wisher found themselves
searching for food near the big oak. Gold,
brown and yellow leaves had fallen from
the tree, so they scraped them away to
uncover the grass beneath.

When Bracken grew bored doing that, he kicked up some leaves just for fun.

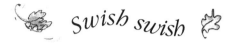 *Swish swish*

"Ouch!"

There was something soft, grey and furry, half-hidden behind a pile of leaves. Unfortunately for Bracken, it was Sylvia Squirrel.

"Clumsy rabbit!" said Sylvia. "Mind where you're going."

"I'm sorry, Sylvia," said Bracken. "I can't see very well . . ." Suddenly he remembered he hadn't seen Wisher for a while. "Wisher! Wisher! Where are you?"

"Boo!" said Wisher.

She was only a few hops away, but her silvery-white fur was hard to see in the mist.

"You scared me!" said Bracken. Then he laughed. He knew Wisher was getting her own back because he'd teased her before.

"Fun and games are all very well," said Sylvia, "but it's time you went home. Your parents will be wondering where you are. Besides, I heard a fox earlier. He wasn't far from here."

Bracken and Wisher looked at each other.

"What does a fox sound like?" asked Bracken.

"A few short barks," said Sylvia. "Now hurry. Off you go."

Bracken and Wisher thanked Sylvia for her warning, and set off for home.

Bracken's Foxy Plan
2

"Stay close," said Bracken, as they hopped through swirling wisps of white.

"I will!" said Wisher.

They both knew how easily they could lose sight of each other, and there was also that fox to worry about! The two young rabbits listened, hoping to hear Bramble, Berry and Fern. But they couldn't hear a sound. Silence filled the misty air.

"Is anyone there?" called Bracken.

Again, they heard nothing.

Wisher felt her ears tingle the way they sometimes did when something was about to happen. Wisher knew she had special powers, but she didn't understand how they worked. Her eldermarr, Primrose Longears, had once told her it was a wonderful gift. Then Wisher heard a familiar voice inside her head:

I whisper a song like the wind in your ear.
Wisher, beware. Wisher, take care!

Wisher frowned.

"What's the matter . . . ?" Bracken began.

He stopped at the sound of three short barks. Bracken and Wisher knew that chilling call. Seconds later, trotting out of the mist, came a big, red FOX!

"What now?" said Wisher. She felt very afraid.

Bracken's thoughts were racing. What would Bramble do? He wished his brother were here!

Then he spotted a clump of thistles.

"Make for those," he whispered. "We'll hide there. Quick!"

The two rabbits dashed for the prickly plants and crouched, trembling with fear.

Bracken and Wisher watched the fox make his way slowly towards them. He had a thick, reddish-brown coat, a bushy tail and a short, pointed snout. Bracken was sure the animal was on their trail, because every now and then he stopped and sniffed. *Sniff, sniff!*

Bracken remembered what Parr had told them all that morning. 'A fox has a fine nose for smelling rabbits.'

It was only a matter of time before this one would find them. They had to do something, but what?

"We'll split up," he whispered to Wisher. "I'll go first. The fox will chase me but I'll outrun him, you'll see! You go home the other way. He can't chase two rabbits at once."

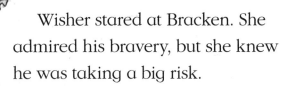

Wisher stared at Bracken. She admired his bravery, but she knew he was taking a big risk.

"No," she said. "He'll catch you!"

"It's our best chance to escape," said Bracken, sounding more confident than he felt. "Trust me, Wisher. My plan will work!"

Before Wisher could stop him, Bracken ran into the open. The fox chased after him.

Bracken was proud of the fact that he was the fastest rabbit in his family, but he'd never run from a fox before.

As he sped along, ears flat, tail bobbing, Bracken was terrified and excited at the same time. Parr and Marr would be horrified if they could see him now. Oh no! thought Bracken. The fox is right behind me. I can hear him panting. Maybe Wisher was right! Oh, help!

Bracken looked around for somewhere to hide. He spotted a holly bush not far away. Can I make it? I must! Bracken darted this way and that, running faster than he'd ever run before, until he reached the holly and dived for safety.

He crouched, still as a stone, his heart
thumping so loudly he was sure the fox
could hear it.

The fox was very cross with himself for
losing sight of the rabbit. It had been only
a jaw's snap away when it had suddenly
vanished. *Sniff, sniff!* He knew the rabbit
was down there somewhere! For a while
he circled the holly, then he lay flat on his
belly, trying to peer through the prickly
leaves. But seeing no sign of the rabbit,
he gave up.

When Bracken dared to move, he
stretched his neck just enough to look
over the edge of his hiding place. He was
very relieved to see the fox trotting away.

Then something else caught his attention.
The mist made it difficult to see clearly,
but he was sure there was something
moving by a fence. The blurry shape was
heading his way! It was a small animal
with silvery-white fur . . .

"Wisher!" cried Bracken, crawling out
from under the holly. "What are you doing
here?"

"I followed you," said Wisher. "I *had* to
know you'd got away."

"You were supposed to go home," said Bracken crossly. "That was my plan . . ."

"Yes, I know," said Wisher. "But you risked being caught to save me. You were SO brave!"

Bracken felt a tingle in his tail. He was pleased to have done something useful, without any help from Bramble. He'd helped Wisher *and* outwitted the fox – all by himself! He thought Bramble would have been proud of him.

"Thanks," he said. "That fox nearly caught me!"

"Come on," said Wisher. "Marr and Parr will be getting worried."

"Yes, Parr will organise a search party if we're not home soon," said Bracken.

"Well, let's get back before he does!" said Wisher.

Through
the
Hedge
3

At Number Five, Fir Tree Walk, Nigel the
rabbit was waiting for his breakfast. Abby,
the little girl who looked after him, was
late this morning. Nigel peered through
the wire netting of his hutch to see if she
was coming down the path, but there was
no sign of her yet. In fact, he couldn't see
much at all.

"How strange!" said Nigel. "A
cloud must have fallen from the sky.
Everything's covered in mist."

To pass the time, and to take his mind off the fact he was hungry, Nigel hopped into his run. When the weather was warm enough, like now, Nigel lived outside in the garden. Abby had moved his run to a fresh patch of lawn where the grass was fresh and green. It took him ten hops to reach the end. He drank from the water bottle clipped to the side of his cage. Then he looked hopefully at the contents of his bright yellow feeding bowl.

There was a scrap of lettuce leaf, left over from yesterday, but it had wilted and didn't look nice to eat. Nigel's tummy rumbled.

"I hope Abby comes soon," he said.

Just then his friend, a Siamese cat called Ming, came to see him. Ming lived in Abby's house and knew everything that went on there.

"It's chaos this morning," said Ming. "Everyone's overslept. Abby says her parents' alarm clock didn't go off, whatever that is, and she must be at school on time. Her dad has a train to catch, whatever that is, and her mum has to be at an office, whatever *that* is, so they're all running about like chickens. I'm not sure what chickens are but I've heard they run about . . ."

"Ming!" said Nigel. "Will Abby remember to feed me before she goes to school?"

"Well . . ." said Ming, giving Nigel a serious look. "The way things are going, it's not likely, in my opinion."

"But I'm starving," said Nigel. "If I don't eat soon, I'll die!"

Ming looked at Nigel's round, plump body.

"I don't think you will . . ." she began.

Abby was running down the garden path.

"Oh, Nigel!" she said, unfastening the latch on his hutch. "Here's your breakfast. Your favourite, Nutty Nibbles. I'll change your water too. I don't have time for a cuddle today. We'll play when I get home, I promise!"

Then Abby shut the wooden door and ran off. By now the mist had cleared a little, and Nigel could see Abby's mum waiting by the car and hear the purr of its engine. He thought it looked like a big, black cat with yellow eyes. The car doors slammed as everyone got in, and the family drove away.

"Peace at last!" said Ming, settling herself on a sunny patch of grass to wash.

"Mmmm!" said Nigel, his cheeks full of Nutty Nibbles. His bowl was packed with delicious food – oats, maize, nuts and sunflower seeds – all the things he liked best. He munched and crunched happily, till he could munch and crunch no more. Then, after a few drops of water, he hopped into his hutch to take a nap. He took a while to make himself a comfortable nest in the sweet-smelling hay which Abby always provided. He was just snuggling down when he noticed the door.

It was ajar.

"Ooo!" said Nigel. His ears twitched. He got up and nudged the door with his nose. One gentle push and it swung open!

Nigel's heart beat a little faster.

This had never happened before.

Suddenly he didn't feel a bit sleepy, so . . .

He hopped outside!

At first, Nigel didn't go far from his hutch. It was strange being in the garden on his own without Abby.

But he soon felt more confident and went right to the middle of the lawn. The grass had been cut short, so there wasn't much to eat. He thought the hedge at the bottom of the garden looked much more interesting. Nigel remembered seeing Abby's dad cutting it – *Snip, snip, snip!* He'd missed some leafy twigs at the bottom. Mmm! thought Nigel. I wonder what they taste like. And he went to see.

When Ming had finished washing she was surprised to see Nigel hopping free. She went down to the end of the garden after him.

"What are you doing?" she said.

"I'm exploring," said Nigel excitedly. "Look, I've found a hole in the hedge!"

"I wouldn't poke your nose through there," said Ming.

36

"Why not?" said Nigel.

"Because there's a Dark Forest on the other side," said Ming. "It's full of wild animals!"

"What are they?" asked Nigel.

Ming rolled her eyes.

"Don't you know *anything?*" she said. "Wild animals are very big and fierce. They have horns growing out of their heads. And sharp teeth and . . . well, they're just terrible hairy beasts!"

Nigel listened carefully. He didn't believe everything Ming told him. After all, she'd been wrong about Abby coming to feed him, hadn't she?

This was his one chance for adventure. He wasn't going to let Ming put him off. He'd made up his mind to explore the Dark Forest, and that was that.

"I'm going," said Nigel. "I'll be back before Abby comes home."

Then he disappeared through the hedge.

A Secret Tunnel
4

"Are you sure this is the right way?"
said Wisher.

Bracken groaned.

"No," he said. "I think we've been
going round in circles! Look, there's
the holly where I hid from the fox."

Wisher looked worried.

"Do you think he's still around?"
she said. "Oh, I wish Marr and Parr
were here!"

"Cheer up," said Bracken. "We'll find our way back. Parr said the mist would clear, remember?"

Wisher nodded. As she did, she felt the ground tremble beneath her paws. She noticed a small mound of freshly-dug earth.

"Did you feel that?" she said.

"Yes," said Bracken. "What is it?"

"I'm not sure," said Wisher slowly. "It could be . . . it might be . . . oh, I hope it's who I think it is!"

"Who?" said Bracken.

Just then, a pointed, whiskery snout pushed its way out through a heap of soil.

"Parsley!" cried Wisher.

"Silly me!" said Bracken. "I should have known it would be you tunnelling down there."

"Lost again?" said Parsley. "You two
are a long way from home."

"Do you know where we are?" said
Wisher.

Parsley's eyesight wasn't good at the
best of times, but on this misty morning
he couldn't see a thing.

"I'm not sure where *this* is," he said. "Come with me. Tunnels are the very best way to get about. I'm sure I can find your burrow."

"Thanks, Parsley," said Wisher. "I'm small enough for your tunnels. I'm not sure about you, Bracken. You're bigger than me."

"Let me try," said Bracken.

Wisher and Parsley watched as Bracken squeezed his head into the hole. He kicked with his back legs and wriggled his bottom. But no matter how hard he tried, Bracken couldn't fit into the tunnel.

"Shall I give you a push?" said Parsley helpfully.

"No!" said Bracken. "I'm stuck."

"You take one leg," Wisher said to Parsley. "I'll grab the other. Ready? Pull!"

"OW!" cried Bracken.

He popped from the hole and they all fell over backwards.

"That settles it," said Wisher. "We can't go with you, Parsley."

"I'll stay," said Parsley cheerfully. "I get lonely by myself."

Bracken got up and brushed himself down. He saw they were standing at a place where three paths met.

The friends couldn't decide which path to take, but then Bracken had an idea.

"I'll toss a stick," he said. "Whichever path it points to, that's the path we'll take. If we're lucky, it will lead us home!"

Bracken threw a stick into the air and it landed, *Splat!* on a muddy path. "Let's go!" he said.

Only Wisher noticed they were leaving a trail of paw prints in the mud. At least if we get lost, we can retrace our tracks, she thought.

As they went along, Parsley told Bracken and Wisher a story.

"Did I ever tell you about the time I found a great fat worm?" he said.

"No," said Wisher. "I don't think you did."

"Well," said Parsley. "I was mending one of my tunnels. It's important to keep tunnels in good order, you know. It stops them falling down. Anyway, I came up for some fresh air in the flowerbed at The Station."

"We went there once," said Wisher. "You showed me where the Red Dragon lived, remember?"

"Quite right," said Parsley. "Now, where was I? Ah, yes. Worms. There, among the flowers, was the biggest worm I'd ever seen."

"What a nice surprise," said Bracken.

"That's what I thought," said Parsley. "I grabbed his tail and pulled. But the worm stretched. On and on. The more I pulled, the longer he grew! Then *Whooosh!* A jet of water knocked me off my feet!"

"Oh no!" said Wisher. "What happened?"

Parsley smiled and shook his head.

"You'll never guess," he said. "The worm wasn't a worm, after all. It was a hosepipe!"

"What's a *hosepipe?*" said Bracken and Wisher.

"People-folk use them for watering plants," Parsley told them. "I won't make that mistake again!"

They all laughed, but as they did, Wisher's ears began to tingle. She looked nervously about, expecting to see the fox, or Burdock the buzzard swoop from the sky. It was still difficult to see anything clearly, but as far as she could tell, they were not in any danger. What's wrong? she wondered. My ears were trying to tell me something.

Then they heard a loud whistle.

Whooo-Wheeep!

"Oh, no!" cried Bracken. "It's the Red Dragon!"

The noisy monster rattled and clattered along the valley.

Bracken and Wisher thought they must have strayed on to the Dragon's tracks, and leapt out of his way. They landed in a very boggy place.

"Ugh!" said Wisher.

"Mud!" said Bracken.

The two rabbits climbed back on to the path.

"Where's the Red Dragon?" said Bracken.

"He's gone," said Parsley. "Don't worry. You weren't in any danger. His tracks are over there."

"The mist is starting to clear," said Wisher.

"Parr said it would," said Bracken. Then he saw that Wisher had a faraway look in her eyes. "What's the matter?"

"I think my ears were trying to warn me about something," she said. "But I don't think it was about the fox, or Burdock, or the Red Dragon."

"You and your ears!" said Bracken. "I expect you're just imagining things."

"You worry too much," said Parsley. "We're fine, aren't we?"

Wisher nodded. Maybe Parsley and Bracken were right.

Not far ahead, they saw higher ground rising from the marsh. Bracken realised he'd brought them to a strange part of the Ripple River Valley, and wished he hadn't trusted his stick to find their way home.

"Let's make for that hill," he said.
"Maybe we'll see more from the top."

They soon discovered that getting
there wouldn't be easy. Growing
around the bottom of the hill were
hawthorn, shrubby trees and brambles.
But Bracken bravely fought his way
through a mass of tangled grass and
weeds where the path was wet and
slippery.

Wisher was glad they were still leaving a trail of tracks. Then Bracken gave a shout:

"Slugs and snails! There's something blocking our way."

"I can't see anything," said Parsley.

Bracken pulled aside a curtain of leaves. Behind it was a crumbling brick wall.

"Let's go back," said Wisher. She didn't like this place.

"Wait!" said Bracken. "There's something here."

"What?" said Parsley.

"A hole," said Bracken. "A huge hole? An enormous burrow!" His words echoed back:

Burrow – burrow – burrow – burrow!

"Please be careful," said Wisher.

Then Parsley took a look.

"This isn't a burrow," he said. It's much too big. No, it's a tunnel! Bracken Longears, you've found a Secret Tunnel!"

The Dark Forest 5

Nigel was exploring the Dark Forest. The trees grew so tall and so straight, Nigel thought their tops might touch the sky. There were rows and rows of them, one after another, and their pine needles littered the forest floor.

"Everything smells different here," said Nigel, sniffing the bark of one tree. "The forest is very big. And very dark. And very quiet." He was beginning to think the world outside his hutch was just a little frightening.

He remembered how Ming had warned him about the wild creatures that lived here. She'd said they were big. She'd told him they were fierce. Terrible beasts with sharp teeth and horns!

Nigel shivered. But he couldn't see or hear any sign of life. No wild animals. No birds. Just trees. Hm! thought Nigel. How disappointing. The Dark Forest isn't very exciting after all.

The silence of the forest was suddenly shattered by a loud buzzing noise.

Buz-z-z-z-z-z-z-z-z-z!

It went on and on. Nigel turned one way then the other, trying to see who or what it could be.

"It's an angry bee!" he said. "Maybe lots of angry bees!"

Then he heard something else. The forest floor vibrated.

Snap, snap, crack!

It was the sound
of dry sticks snapping
under pounding
hooves. An animal
with big antlers was
heading his way!

"Oh no!" cried Nigel.
"A w-w-w-wild animal! A
f-f-f-fierce beast. I'm off!"

Nigel ran through the forest as fast
as his legs could carry him. Through the
trees, under a fence and across a wide,
open space. He'd never run so far or fast
in his life! When he could go no further,
Nigel stopped to hide beside a huge pile
of logs. He looked around. There was no
sign of the scary creature
with horns, but he could
still hear the buzzing noise.
It was much louder now.

Buz-z-z-z-z-z-z-z-z-z!

"I want to go home!" said Nigel.

As he plucked up the courage to leave, there came a loud

CRA-A-A-A-CK! followed by silence. Then *WHOOOSH! SWISH!* A fir tree crashed to the ground.

"What's happening?" said Nigel.

"Bees buzz . . ." he said. "I know that. And trees don't usually fall by themselves. But what if bees in the Dark Forest are very big? They sound big and angry to me! Did they make the tree fall down? Oh, why didn't I listen to Ming? She told me not to come. I've been such a silly rabbit!"

A tear trickled down Nigel's nose and plopped on the ground. He wondered if he would ever see Ming again. He missed Abby too, and his hutch and . . .

Buz-z-z-z-z-z-z-z-z-z!

The buzzing noise started again, only this time it was closer.

"The bees are after me!" said Nigel. "I must find somewhere to hide."

He looked around, then spotted something partly overgrown with weeds. It looked like the entrance to a cave.

"Just the place!" said Nigel, and he made a dash for it.

"Now this is what I call a tunnel!" said Parsley.

They were standing just inside Bracken's secret tunnel.

"I can see daylight at the far end," said Bracken. "Let's see where it goes."

"It's spooky," said Wisher. "There might be something in there."

"Like what?" said Bracken.

"Anything," said Wisher. "A dangerous animal. Maybe a fox! My ears are tingling again. I *know* something's wrong."

"Oh, you're just scared," said Bracken. "Come on. It might take us home."

"Bracken's right," said Parsley. "If we don't try, we won't find out. Up the Burrowers!"

"Okay," said Wisher. "But I don't like it."

After one last look at their muddy tracks outside, she followed Bracken and Parsley into the tunnel.

It was cold and damp. Water trickled down the walls and they hopped over loose rocks along the way.

Maybe Wisher was right, thought Bracken. This wasn't such a good idea. He imagined a hairy monster lying in wait for them. And he remembered what Marr had said that morning: "Silly rabbits have careless habits!"

Parsley was thoroughly enjoying his walk through the tunnel, although he *was* worried about the poor state of the brickwork.

"It's falling to bits!" he said, tripping over a stone. "That's the thing about tunnels. You have to look after them."

"Not far now," said Bracken. He couldn't wait to reach the other end. But as he said it, they heard a buzzing noise ahead.

Buz-z-z-z-z-z-z-z-z!

"Wha-wha-what's that?" said Wisher.

"I can't see anything," said Parsley.

Bracken gulped. They were about to be attacked by a horrible beast – and it was all his fault!

"Probably n-n-nothing to w-w-worry about," he said, although he wasn't sure this was true.

As they neared the end of the tunnel, they could see tall trees, and the buzzing sound grew louder.

Buz-z-z-z-z-z-z-z-Z-Z!

Wisher's ears tingled again.

"Bracken," she said. "There is something wrong. I know it . . ."

Bracken didn't get a chance to reply, because a small animal suddenly charged into the tunnel. Bracken, Wisher and Parsley froze as it raced towards them.

Then the creature skidded to a stop. For a moment or two, all four stared at one another in silence.

Bracken, the first to recover, was surprised to find himself nose to nose with a large black-and-white rabbit.

Wisher's Warning

6

"Hello," said Bracken. "I'm Bracken Longears. Who are you?"

"I'm Nigel," said Nigel. "Don't go out there. There's a swarm of bees. Big ones. Listen! You can hear them buzzing."

"How big?" said Parsley. "I've seen lots of bees. They don't scare me!"

"Er, well . . ." said Nigel. "I haven't *seen* them."

"Let's go back anyway," said Wisher. "My ears are warning me about something. I just don't know what."

Bracken was confused. Nigel was scared of some bees he hadn't seen, and Wisher was worried about things that *might* happen.

"I think we should go on," he said.

"So do I," said Parsley.

"Stop!" said Wisher.

Bracken rolled his eyes.

"What now?" he said impatiently.

"I can hear a voice inside my head," she said.

"Wisher goes a bit funny sometimes," Bracken told Nigel, even though he could see she was serious.

Rocks like leaves in autumn fall,
Inside a secret tunnel wall!

From somewhere deep inside the tunnel, they heard a dull THUD, followed by the rumble of tumbling rocks. Seconds later, a swirling cloud of dust came towards them.

"Help!" cried Nigel.

"Take cover!" said Parsley.

"Run!" shouted Wisher.

"NOW!" cried Bracken.

The four raced from the tunnel and didn't stop running until they'd reached the forest. There they stopped by a tall fir tree. Bracken, Wisher and Nigel rubbed dirt from their eyes. Parsley brushed dust from his velvety coat.

"Phew!" said Nigel. "We got out just in time."

"It wouldn't have happened in one of my tunnels," said Parsley.

"Thanks, Wisher," said Bracken. "Your ears were right!"

"I'm glad we didn't turn back," said Wisher.

"So am I," said Bracken. "The tunnel's blocked. We'll have to go on now, won't we?"

Wisher nodded.

"Where are you going?" asked Nigel.

"We're trying to find our way home," said Bracken. "We're lost."

"I want to go home too," said Nigel.

"Where's that?" said Wisher.

Nigel looked around.

"I don't know," he said. "I've crawled through a hedge and been chased by a wild animal! I've run from bees . . ."

"So, you're lost?" said Parsley.

"Yes," said Nigel. "I suppose I am. I have to get back before Abby returns from school. And Ming will be missing me by now."

Bracken, Wisher and Parsley had no idea what Nigel was talking about, but they offered to help immediately. Bracken remembered the time he and Bramble had helped a lost chick find its mother. This time *he'd* be in charge!

"Our only clue is a hedge . . ." said Bracken, thinking aloud. "Well, at least we know what that is! Come on. It will be dark soon."

And they set off through the trees.

The Beast with Yellow Eyes
7

"Where's Nigel?" cried Abby. "He's gone!"

Ming had waited for Nigel to return all afternoon. She greeted Abby when she got back from school, but couldn't think how to show her what had happened. Ming was worried about Nigel too. It was getting dark. Lights glowed from the windows at Number Five, Fir Tree Walk, and lanterns lit up the garden.

Ming watched Abby's dad walk slowly down the path, peering into plants and flowerbeds.

"No sign of him," he said.

Ming caught sight of Abby's mum. She was on her hands and knees, shining a torch under the shed at the bottom of the garden. And she was near the hedge.

Ming hurried down
the lawn and sat by
the hedge at the place
where Nigel had
squeezed through.
Then she threw back
her head and yowled.

"ME-OW-OW-OW-OW!"

"What's the matter?" cried Abby. She
looked at Ming, then she saw the gap.
There was a scrap of Nigel's fur still
clinging to a leaf.

"Mum! Dad!" cried
Abby. "Look. Nigel
went through here.
He's in the forest!"
She stroked
Ming. "Thank
you, Ming.
You're a very
clever cat!"

Ming purred and purred. Her idea had worked. I hope they find Nigel soon, she thought, as she watched the family jump into their car. Two bright yellow headlights lit up the drive, and they were off down the road to the forest.

Bracken, Wisher, Parsley and Nigel hurried through the Dark Forest, searching for the hedge. The buzzing noise had stopped now, but they still kept a look-out for the wild animal with horns that Nigel had told them about. The four friends chatted happily as they went along.

"Where do you live?" Nigel asked Bracken.

"Down a burrow, of course," said Bracken. "Our home is near the River Ripple."

"What's a burrow?" said Nigel.

Bracken couldn't believe his ears.

"It's a small tunnel," he said. "We live underground. I thought all rabbits did."

"I don't," said Nigel.

"Where do you live?" said Wisher.

"In a hutch, of course," said Nigel.

"*A what?*" said the others.

"A hutch," said Nigel. "It's like a shed, only smaller. Abby cleans it every day.

And she grooms my fur with a brush.

I like being brushed.

It tickles!"

Bracken, Wisher
and Parsley tried hard to
understand everything Nigel was
telling them.

"Who is Abby?" said Bracken.

"She's the little girl who looks after
me," said Nigel.

Bracken looked at Nigel in
amazement.

"You live with . . . people-folk?"
he said.

"Yes," said Nigel. "I thought all
rabbits did."

"No," said Bracken. "They do not!
We live with Marr and Parr."

"And Bramble, Berry and Fern," said
Wisher.

"Who are rabbits," added Parsley, just
to make things clear.

"How strange!" said Nigel. "I think I'd get bored living with rabbits. Abby and I have fun playing in the garden. Sometimes I'm allowed inside her house! I sit on her bed while she plays on her computer. My friend, Ming, told me what it was. Ming knows everything. She's a cat. I hope I see her soon."

"And I hope we find your hedge soon," said Bracken. "The forest is so big. I can't see anything but trees."

Nigel's tummy rumbled. It seemed a long time since breakfast.

"I'm hungry," he said.

"So am I," said Wisher and Bracken.

"Me too," said Parsley. "I'd give anything for a worm."

"Ugh!" said Nigel. "You eat worms?"

"Mmmmm!" said Parsley. "Just thinking about them makes me happy. What do you eat?"

"Nutty Nibbles!" said Nigel. "They're my favourite. Abby brings them in a box. I think I left some in my bowl."

Bracken laughed. "We find our own food," he said. "Marr taught us how to find the right plants. But there's nothing to eat around here. Not one blade of grass!"

Later, when the four tired animals thought they'd never find their way out of the gloomy forest, Bracken saw a shaft of sunlight. The red sun was slipping behind some trees and beyond there was a green, open space.

"Look!" cried Bracken, running ahead and flipping a somersault. "Grass, grass, grass!"

"Hooray!" shouted Wisher.
"Dandelions!"

"Got you!" cried Parsley, grabbing a worm. He gobbled it up in one go.

Nigel looked on helplessly. He didn't know what to do.

"Here," said Wisher, offering him a dandelion leaf. "Try one of these."

"Thanks," said Nigel, and took a few nibbles. But all of a sudden he found he'd lost his appetite. "I just want to go home."

He looked very sad. Nigel depended on people-folk for everything, and now he needed them to get him home.

"We want to go home too," said Bracken gently. "Don't worry, Nigel. We won't leave you. Look, there's a path. Maybe it will take us to your hedge."

The moon rose high in the starry sky.
Bracken led his rescue party along a
wide, smooth path through the Dark
Forest. He looked about nervously,
remembering how Parr had warned
them about animals that hunted at night.

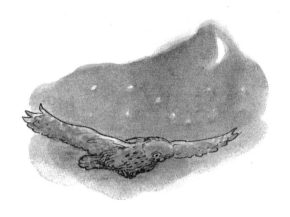

He and Wisher should have been back ages ago, and Parr and Marr would be worrying their whiskers off. But now they were on a dangerous mission! The sooner they got Nigel safely home, the better.

Without warning, an owl swooped low and silently from behind. Wisher heard its wing beats just in time.

"Down! Get down!" she shouted.

Bracken and Wisher dived under
a bush at the side of the road. Parsley
disappeared down a hole.

Nigel sat in the middle of the road,
wondering what all the fuss was about.

"Where are you?" he shouted. "Are we
playing hide-and-seek?"

When Bracken was sure the owl had
gone, he crawled out from his hiding
place.

"No, Nigel," he said. "We are not
playing a game. That was an owl. Don't
you know owls eat rabbits? You were
lucky he didn't carry you off!"

Nigel shook his head. It hadn't
occurred to him he was in any danger

Wisher looked at Nigel. He was quite
large. She doubted the owl could have
picked him up, but she didn't say so.

"I think you're all very brave," said
Nigel. "I couldn't look after myself
like you do."

"That's why I prefer to travel by tunnel," said Parsley. "It's much safer. You know where you are with tunnels. In one end. Out the other."

"Except when they're blocked in the middle," Wisher reminded him.

"Ah, yes," said Parsley, remembering the secret tunnel. "But I always look after MY tunnels . . ."

Parsley broke off. A deep roaring sound suddenly filled the air.

"Wh-wh-what's that?" said Bracken.

Then everything happened so fast that he couldn't be sure what was going on. Later, when he'd had time to think, he remembered seeing two enormous yellow eyes, coming fast down the road. At first, he thought the owl had returned. But these eyes were much bigger. Scarily big! Maybe it was the animal who'd chased Nigel?

Bracken froze in the glare of its lights.

It roared closer and closer. Bracken shut his eyes tight. He was sure they'd all be eaten by the Beast with Yellow Eyes! Next thing he knew, there were people-folk shouting. He opened his eyes, and saw a little girl running towards them.

"Mum! Dad! Nigel's here!" she cried happily. "Oh Nigel, it's Abby. Come to me!" Then she scooped Nigel into her arms and carried him away.

The last Bracken, Wisher and Parsley saw of Nigel, he was peeping over Abby's shoulder looking back at them. They couldn't be sure, but they thought they heard him call out:

"Thank you! Goodbye!"

Then he was gone, carried away by the Beast with Yellow Eyes.

Tracks, Trails and Rabbit Tales
8

Back at the Longears' warren, Barley and
Mellow were worried out of their wits.
When the mist had cleared, Barley sat
on his favourite tree stump to keep watch.
He was still there when Sylvia Squirrel
came along.

"Have you seen Bracken and Wisher?"
said Barley. "They've been missing since
this morning."

"I *did* see them over by the big oak,"
said Sylvia. "Bracken bumped into me!
It wasn't really his fault because it was
so misty. I could hardly see my own tail!

87

I told them both to hurry
home. Didn't they
arrive? Oh, dear!
Children can be such
a worry, can't they?"

"Yes, yes, thank you, Sylvia," said
Barley. "Did you see where they went?"

Sylvia waved a paw in the direction
of a path near the oak.

"I think they went that way," she said.

Barley raced home to organise a
search for the missing pair.

"Bramble and Berry, go with Marr," he
said. "Fern, come with me. We'll start over
by the big oak.
Everyone,
keep your
eyes open!
Meet back
here before
dark."

Fern was pleased Parr had chosen her to go with him. She was good at following tracks and trails. As they hurried along a footpath, she remembered the time she and Berry had followed paw prints in the snow. It had got Berry into trouble – he'd been carried off by the Red Dragon!

Barley and Fern soon arrived at the place where three paths met. Fern spotted two sets of rabbit tracks, but she was puzzled about a third set of paw prints.

"Do you know who those belong to, Parr?" she said.

Barley scratched his ear.

"Hm?" he said. "Smaller than a rabbit. Bigger than a mouse. An animal with five long claws. Could be a mole?"

"Parsley!" cried Fern. "It must be Bracken, Wisher and Parsley."

"Come on," said Barley. "Let's go!"

It was easy to follow the tracks in the mud. But Barley and Fern found themselves in strange surroundings. The path took them around a wet, boggy marsh.

"I've lived most of my life in the Ripple River Valley," said Barley. "And I've never been here before."

Fern, who was leading the way,

followed the paw prints through long grass and tangled bushes. Suddenly they came to some trailing ivy and. . .

"Bugs and beetles!" she cried.

"What's the matter?" said Barley.

"A tunnel!" said Fern. "Look. Their tracks stop here. I think Bracken, Wisher and Parsley went in there!"

Barley took a few hops inside. He called and called, but there was no reply – only their names came echoing back.

BRACKEN! WISHER! PARSLEY!

Together he and Fern peered into the gloom. They were used to the darkness of a burrow, which smelled of earth and tree roots. Barley wrinkled his nose, sniffing the air. *Sniff, sniff!* Then he sneezed. *Atishoooo!* The sound vibrated along the tunnel walls and boomed back, louder than before. *ATISHOOOO!*

"The tunnel's full of dust!" he said.

They went on a little further, but their way was blocked by a pile of fallen rocks.

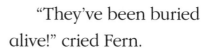

"They've been buried alive!" cried Fern.

"Oh, buttercups!" said Barley, tugging his ears. "I feel dizzy. I can't think! We must do something, Fern."

He took a deep breath and tried to calm himself. "We don't know what's happened, do we? Bracken, Wisher and Parsley may be trapped on the other side. We'll need help moving all these rocks. I'm sure my friend, Blinker Badger, will lend a paw. Come on, let's go back and tell the others."

Bracken, Wisher and Parsley waited until the Beast with Yellow Eyes was out of sight. He was a scary-looking creature with red eyes at the back of his head! Then they hurried along the road.

To their surprise and delight, it led them to a place near the river. Long before they saw it, they could hear the sound of water swishing over rocks.

"The river!" cried Bracken.

"Look," shouted Wisher. "There's the wooden bridge. We're nearly home!"

"At last!" said Parsley.

"Race you to the bridge," said Bracken. "Ready? One, two, three . . . go!"

"You always win!" said Wisher.

And he did.

Later that evening, Barley and Mellow Longears, Bramble, Berry, Bracken, Fern, Wisher and Parsley sat under a starry sky. Blinker Badger was there too, after Barley had asked for his help. Luckily, as things turned out, it hadn't been needed.

"Come on, Bracken," said Blinker. "Tell us what happened today. I like a good story!"

There was a lot to remember, so Wisher and Parsley helped Bracken with the details. Everyone was interested in Nigel.

"You say he lives with people-folk?" said Barley. "Whatever next!"

"A rabbit that doesn't know what a burrow is?" said Berry. "Are you sure Nigel was a rabbit, Bracken?"

Mellow smiled. She couldn't imagine a better life for a rabbit than living here in the Ripple River Valley.

"We have everything we need," she said. "Grass in the meadow. Fruit from the hedgerow. Water from the river. What more could a rabbit wish for?"

"I can think of a few things," said Barley, looking up at the sky. "I wish owls and Burdock the buzzard lived somewhere else!"

"And foxes!" said Bracken. "I had to run fast today, I can tell you."

Mellow gave Bracken a look.

"I'm glad I wasn't there to see you," she said. "I'd have turned white with fright."

Bramble gave Bracken a friendly nudge.

"You're getting as brave as me!" he said.

Bracken's tail tingled with pride.

That night, when Mellow came to say goodnight, she found Bracken thinking about his new friend, Nigel.

"Nigel's life is very different to ours," said Bracken. "I would hate to live in a hutch."

"Yes," said Mellow. "But he's happy. That's all that matters. Home is home wherever or whatever it is."

Bracken yawned.

"You're right," he said sleepily. "Nigel couldn't wait to get home to Abby, Ming and . . ."

"Sleep well," said Mellow. "Thank the stars you're safely home too!"